You Can't Catch Me!

Written by Alison Hawes

Illustrated by David Roberts

"Run, run as fast as you can.

You can't catch me,

I'm the **running** man!"

3

"Jump, jump as fast as you can.
You can't catch me,
I'm the **jumping** man!"

"Hop, hop as fast as you can.
You can't catch me,
I'm the **hopping** man!"

"Skip, skip as fast as you can.

You can't catch me,

I'm the **skipping** man!"

"Run, run as fast as you can.

You can't catch me,

I'm the **running** man!"

"Walk, walk as fast as you can.
I'm IT now,"
said the walking man.